SPACEBRED GENERATIONS

SPACEBRED GENERATIONS

CLIFFORD D. SIMAK

WILDSIDE PRESS

SPACEBRED GENERATIONS

"Spacebred Generations" (also published as "Target Generation") originally appeared in *Science Fiction Plus*, August 1953 issue.

This edition has been published in 2009 by Wildside Press, LLC.
www.wildsidebooks.com

SPACEBRED GENERATIONS

THERE had been silence—for many generations. Then the silence ended.

The Mutter came at "dawn."

The Folk awoke, crouching in their beds, listening to the Mutter. For had it not been spoken that one day would come the Mutter? And that the Mutter would be the beginning of the End?

Jon Hoff awoke, and Mary Hoff, his wife.

They were the only two within their cubicle, for they had no children. They were not yet allowed a child. Before they could have a child, before there would be room for it, the elderly Joshua must die, and knowing this they had waited for his death, guilty at their unspoken prayer that he soon must die—willing him to die so they might have a child.

The Mutter came and ran throughout the Ship. Then the bed in which Jon and Mary crouched spun upward from the floor and crashed against the wall, pinning them against the humming metal, while all the other furniture—chest and chairs and table—came crashing from floor to wall, where it came to rest, as if the wall suddenly had become the floor and the floor the wall.

The Holy Picture dangled from the ceiling, which a moment before had been the other wall, hung there for a moment, swaying in the air; then it, too, crashed downward.

In that moment the Mutter ended and there was silence once again—but not the olden silence, for although there was no sound one could reach out and pinpoint, there were many sounds—a feeling, if not a hearing, of the sounds of surging power, of old machinery stirring back to life, of an old order, long dormant, taking over once again.

Jon Hoff crawled out part way from beneath the bed, then straightened on his arms, using his back to lift the bed so his wife could crawl out, too. Free of the bed, they stood on the wall-that-had-become-a-floor and saw the litter of the furniture, which had not been theirs alone, but had been used and then passed down to them through many generations.

For there was nothing wasted; there was nothing thrown away. That was the law—or one of many laws—that you could not waste, that you could not throw away. You used everything there was, down to the last shred of its utility. You ate only enough food—no more, no less. You drank only enough water—no more, no less. You used the same air over and over again—literally the same air. The wastes of your body went into the converter to be changed into something that you, or someone else, would use again. Even the dead—you used the dead again. And there had been many dead in the long generations from the First Beginning. In months to come, some day perhaps not too distant now, Joshua would be added to the dead, would give over his body to the converter for the benefit of his fellow-folk, would return, finally and irrevocably, the last of all that he had taken from the community, would pay the last debt of all his debts—and would give Jon and Mary the right to have a child.

For there must be a child, thought Jon, standing there amidst the wreckage—there must be a child to whom he could pass on the Letter and the Reading.

There was a law about the Reading, too. You did not read because reading was an evil art that came from the Beginning and the Folk had, in the Great Awakening, back in the dimness of Far Past, ferreted out this evil among many other evils and had said it must not be.

So it was an evil thing that he must pass on, an evil art, and yet there was the charge and pledge—the charge of his long-dead father had put upon him, the pledge that he had made. And something else as well: the nagging feeling that the law was wrong.

However, the laws were never wrong. There was a reason for them all. A reason for the way they lived and for the Ship and how the Ship had come to be and for those who peopled it.

Although, come to think of it, he might not pass the letter on. He might be the one who would open it, for it said on the outside of the envelope that it was to be opened in emergency. And this, Jon Hoff told himself, might be emergency—when the silence had been broken by the Mutter and the floor became a wall and the wall a floor.

Now there were voices from the other cubicles, frightened voices that cried out, and other voices that shrieked with terror, and the thin, high crying of the children.

"Jon," said Mary Hoff, "that was the Mutter. The End will be coming now."

"We do not know," said Jon. "We shall have to wait and see. We do not know the End."

"They say . . ." said Mary, and Jon thought that was the way it always was.

They *say*. They *say*. They *say*.

It was spoken; it was not read nor written.

And he heard his dead father speaking once again; the memory of how he had spoken long ago came back.

The brain and the memory will play you false, for the memory will forget a thing and twist it. But the written word will stay forever as it was written down. It does not forget and does not change its meaning. You can depend upon the written word.

"They say," said Mary, "that the End will come swiftly when we hear the Mutter. That the stars will no longer move but will stand still in the blackness, and that is a sure sign the End is near at hand."

And, he wondered, the end of what? The end of us? The end of the Ship? The end of the stars themselves? Or, perhaps, the end of everything, of the Ship and stars and the great blackness in which the stars were spinning.

He shuddered to think of the end of the Folk or of the Ship, not so much that the Ship should end or that the Folk should end, but that the beautiful, efficient, well-balanced order in which they lived should end. For it was a marvelous thing that every function should be so ordered that there always would be enough for the Folk to live on, with never any surplus. No surplus of food or water or air, or of the Folk themselves, for you could not have a child until someone assigned against the coming of that child should die.

There were footsteps running in the corridors outside the cubicles and excited shouting, and suddenly there was someone pounding on the door.

"Jon! Jon!" the voice shouted. "The stars are standing still!"

"I knew it!" Mary cried. "I told you, Jon. It is as it was spoken."

Pounding on the door!

And the door was where it should have been, where a door logically should be, where you could walk straight out of it to the corridor instead of climbing the now useless ladder that ran ridiculously to it from the wall-that-used-to-be-the-floor.

Why didn't I think of that before? he asked himself. Why

didn't I see that it was poor planning to climb to a door that opened in the ceiling?

Maybe, he thought—maybe this is the way it should have been all the time. Maybe the way it had been before was wrong. As the laws might well be wrong.

"I'm coming, Joe," said Jon.

He strode to the door and opened it, and he saw that what had been the wall of the corridor was now the floor and that many doors were opening into it directly from the cubicles and that folks were running up and down the corridor, and he thought: We can take down the ladders now, since we have no use for them. We can feed them into the converter and that will give us the margin that we never have.

Joe gripped him by the arm. "Come with me," he said.

They went to one of the topsy-turvy observation blisters. The stars were standing still.

Exactly as it had been spoken, the stars were still.

It was a frightening thing, for now you could see that the stars were not simply spinning lights that seemed to move against the flatness of a dead-black curtain, but that they were hanging in an emptiness that took the pit out of your stomach and made you gasp and clutch the metal of the ports, fighting to keep your balance, fighting off the light-headedness that came upon you as you stared into a gulf you could not understand.

There were no games that "day," there were no hikes, there was no revelry in the amusement lounge.

There were knots of frightened people talking. There was praying in the chapel where hung the largest of the Holy Pictures, showing the Tree and the Flowers and the River and the House far off, with a Sky that had clouds in it and a Wind you could not see, but only knew was there. There was a picking up and a straightening up of the cubicles in preparation for a "night" of sleeping and a rehanging once again of the Holy Pictures that were the prized possession of each cubicle. There was a taking down of ladders.

Mary Hoff rescued the Holy Picture from the debris on the floor. Jon stood one of the chairs against the wall and hung it upon the wall-that-once-had-been-the-floor and wondered how it happened that each of the Holy Pictures was a little different from all the others. And it was the first time he had ever wondered that.

The Hoffs' Holy Picture had a Tree in it, too, and there were Sheep beneath the Tree and a Fence and Brook, and in the corner of the picture there were some tiny Flowers, and, of course, the Grass that ran up to the Sky.

After he had hung the picture and Mary had gone off to another cubicle to talk in horror-stricken, old-wife fashion with some of the other women, Jon went down the corridor, strolling as casually as he could so that no one would notice him, so that no one would mark any hurry in him.

But there was hurry in him—a sudden, terrible hurry that tried to push him on like two hands against his back.

He tried to look as if he were doing nothing more than genteelly killing time. It was easy for him, for that was all he'd done his entire life, all that any of them had ever done. Except the few, the lucky or unlucky ones, whichever way you might look at it, who had the hereditary jobs—tending the hydroponic gardens or the cattle pens or the poultry flocks.

But most of them, thought Jon, loitering his way along, had done no more than become expert in the art of killing time. Like himself and Joe, with their endless chess games and the careful records that they kept of every move they made, of every move and game. And the hours they spent in analyzing their play from the records that they made, carefully annotating each decisive move. And why not? he asked himself—why not record and annotate the games? What else was there to do? What else?

There were no people now in the corridor, and it had grown dimmer, for now there were only occasional light bulbs to drive back the darkness. Years of bulb-snatching to keep the living cubicles supplied had nearly stripped the Ship.

He came to an observation blister and ducked into it, crouching just inside of it, waiting patiently and watching back along his trail. He waited for the one who might have followed him and he knew there would be no one, but there might be someone and he couldn't take the chance.

No one came, and he went on again, coming to the broken-down escalator which went to the central levels, and here, once again, there was something different. Always before, as he had climbed level after level, he had steadily lost weight, lost the pull against his feet, had swum rather than walked toward the center of the Ship. But this time there was no loss of weight, this time there was no swimming. He trudged broken escalator after broken escalator for all the sixteen decks.

He went in darkness now, for here the bulbs were entirely gone, snatched or burned out over many years. He felt his way upward, with his hand along the guide rails, feeling the cross-draft of the corridors that plunged down the great Ship's length.

He came at last to the proper level and felt his way along until he came to the hiding place, a dispensary room with a pharmaceutical locker against one wall.

He found the proper drawer and pulled it open, and his hand went in and found the three things that he knew were there—the Letter, the Book, and a bulb.

He ran his hand along the wall until he found the outlet, and when he found it, he inserted the bulb and there was light in the tiny room, light upon the dust that lay across the floor and along the counter tops, light upon the wash basin and the sink, the empty cabinets with their idly open doors.

He laid the Letter face up beneath the light and read the words that were printed in block letters:

TO BE OPENED ONLY IN EMERGENCY.

He stood there for a long time, considering. There had been the Mutter. The stars were standing still.

Emergency, he thought. This is emergency.

For had it not been spoken that when the Mutter came and the stars stood still the End was near at hand?

And if the End was near at hand, then it was emergency.

He lifted the Letter in his hand and held it, hesitating. When he opened it, that would be the end of it.

There would be no more handing down—no more of the Letter and the Reading. For this was the moment toward which the Letter had traveled down through time, from father to son for many generations.

Slowly he turned the Letter over and ran a thumbnail along the sealed edge, and the dry wax cracked open and the flap sprang loose.

He reached in and took the message out and spread it flat upon the counter top underneath the lamp.

He read, his lips moving to form whispered words, reading as one must read who had spelled out the slow meaning of his words from an ancient dictionary:

> To the son of my son many times removed:
> They will have told you and by this time you may well believe that the ship is a way of life, that it started in a myth and moves toward a legend and that there is no meaning to be sought within its actuality and no purpose.
> It would be fruitless for me to try to tell you the meaning or the purpose of the ship, for, while these words are true, by themselves, they will have little weight against the perversion of the truth, which by the time you read this may have reached the stature of religion.
> But there is purpose in the ship, although even now, as this is written, the purpose has been lost, and as the ship plunges on its way it will remain not only lost, but buried beneath the weight of human rationalizing.
> In the day that this is read there will be explanations of the ship and the people in it, but there will be no knowledge in the explanations.
> To bring the ship to its destination there must be knowledge. There is a way that knowledge may be gained. I, who will be dead, whose body will have gone back into a plant long eaten, a piece of cloth long worn out, a molecule of oxygen, a pinch of fertilizer, have preserved that knowledge for you. On the second sheet of this letter are the directions for the acquiring of that knowledge.
> I charge you to acquire that knowledge and to use it, that the minds and lives which launched the ship, and the others who kept it going, and those who even now reside within its walls may not have used themselves, nor dedicated themselves, in vain, that the dream of Man may not die somewhere far among the stars.
> You will have learned by the time you read this, even to a greater degree than I know it today, that nothing must be wasted, nothing must be thrown away, that all resources must be guarded and husbanded against a future need.
> And that the ship not reach its destination, that it not serve its purpose, would be a waste so great as to stun the imagination. It would be a terrible waste of thousands of lives, the waste of knowledge and of hope.
> You will not know my name, for my name by the time you read this will be gone with the hand that drives the pen, but my words will still live on and the knowledge in them and the charge.

I sign myself, your ancestor.

And there was a scrawl that Jon could not make out.

He let the Letter drop to the dust-laden countertop, and words from the Letter hammered in his brain.

A ship that started in a myth and moved toward a legend. But that was wrong, the Letter said. There was a purpose and there was a destination.

A destination? What was that? The Book, he thought—the Book will tell what destination is.

With shaking hands he hauled the Book out of the drawer and opened it to *D* and followed down the columns with an unsteady finger: desquamative, dessert, destinate, destination—

Destination (*n*). The place set for the end of a journey, or to which something is sent; a place or point aimed at.

The Ship had a destination. The Ship was *going somewhere*. The day would come when it would reach the place that it was going. And that would be the End, of course. The Ship was going somewhere.

But how? Did the Ship move?

He shook his head in disbelief. That the Ship moved was unbelievable. It was the stars, not the Ship, that moved.

There must be, he felt certain, another explanation. He picked up the Letter's second sheet and read it through, but didn't understand it all, for his brain was tired and befuddled. He put the Letter and the Book and the bulb back in the drawer. He closed the drawer and fled.

They had not noticed his absence in the lower level, and he moved among them, trying to be one of them again, trying to pick up the old cloak of familiarity and wrap it around his sudden nakedness—but he was not one of them.

A terrible knowledge had made him not one of them—the knowledge that the Ship had a purpose and a destination—that it had started somewhere and was going somewhere and that when it got where it was going that would be the End, not of the Folk, nor of the Ship, but only of the Journey.

He went to the lounge and stood for a moment just inside the doorway. Joe was playing chess with Pete, and a swift anger flared within him at the thought that Joe would play with someone else, for Joe had not played chess with anyone but him for many, many years. But the anger dropped quickly from him, and he looked at the chessmen for the first time, really saw them for the first time, and he saw that they were idle hunks of carven wood and that they had no part in this new world of the Letter and the Purpose.

George was sitting by himself playing solitaire, and some of the others were playing poker with the metal counters they called "money," although why they called it money was more than anyone could tell. It was just a name, they said, as the Ship was the name for the ship and the Stars were what the stars were called. Louise and Irma were sitting in one corner listening to an old, almost worn-out recording of a song, and the shrill, pinched voice of the woman who sang screeched across the room:

"My love has gone to the stars,
He will be away for long..."

Jon walked into the room, and George looked up from the cards.

"We've been looking for you," George said.

"I went for a walk," said Jon. "A long walk. On the center levels. It's all wrong up there. It's up, not in. You climb all the way."

"The stars have not moved all day," said George.

Joe turned his head and said, "The stars won't move again. This is as it was spoken. This is the beginning of the End."

"What is the End?" asked Jon.

"I don't know," said Joe and went back to his game.

The End, Jon thought. And none of them know what the End will be, just as they do not know what a ship is, or what money is, or the stars.

"We are meeting," said George. Jon nodded.

He should have known that they would meet. They'd meet for comfort and security. They'd tell the Story once again and they'd pray before the Picture. And I? he thought. And I?

He swung from the room and went out into the corridor, thinking that it might have been best if there'd been no Letter and no Book, for then he'd still be one of them and not a naked stranger standing by himself—not a man torn with wondering which was right, the Story or the Letter.

He found his cubicle and went into it. Mary was there, stretched out on the bed, with the pillows piled beneath her head and the dim bulb burning.

"There you are," she said.

"I went for a walk," said Jon.

"You missed the meal," said Mary. "Here it is."

He saw it on the table and went there, drawing up a chair. "Thanks," he said.

She yawned. "It was a tiring day," she said. "Everyone was so excited. They are meeting."

There was the protein yeast, the spinach and the peas, a thick slice of bread and a bowl of soup, tasty with mushrooms and herbs. And the water bottle, with the carefully measured liquid.

He bent above the soup bowl, spooning the food into his mouth.

"You aren't excited, dear. Not like the rest."

He lifted his head and looked at her. Suddenly he wondered if he might not tell her, but thrust the thought swiftly to one side, afraid that in his longing for human understanding he finally would tell her.

He must watch himself, he thought.

For the telling of it would be proclaimed heresy, the denying of the Story, of the Myth and the Legend. And once she had heard it, she, like the others, would shrink from him and he'd see the loathing in her eyes.

With himself it was different, for he had lived on the fringe of heresy for almost all his life, ever since that day his father had talked to him and told him of the Book. For the Book itself was a part of heresy.

"I have been thinking," he said, and she asked, "What is there to think about?"

And what she said was true, of course. There was nothing to think about. It was all explained, all neat and orderly. The Story told of the Beginning and the beginning of the End. And there was nothing, absolutely nothing for one to think about.

There had been chaos, and out of the chaos order had been born in the shape of the Ship, and outside the Ship there was chaos still. It was only within the Ship that there was order and efficiency and law—or the many laws, the waste not, want not law and all the other laws. There would be an End, but the End was something that was still a mystery, although there still was hope, for with the Ship had been born the Holy Pictures and these in themselves were a symbol of that hope, for within the picture were the symbolism values of other ordered places (bigger ships, perhaps) and all of these symbol values had come equipped with names, with Tree and Book and Sky and Clouds and other things one could not see, but knew were there, like the Wind and Sunshine.

The Beginning had been long ago, so many generations back that the stories and the tales and folklore of the mighty men and women of those long-gone ages pinched out with other shadowy men and women still misty in the background.

"I was scared at first," said Mary, "but I am scared no longer. This is the way that it was spoken, and there is nothing we can do except to know it is for the best."

He went on eating, listening to the sound of passing feet, to the sound of voices going past the door.

Now there was no hurry in the feet, no terror in the voices. It hadn't taken long, he thought, for the Folk to settle down. Their ship had been turned topsy-turvy, but it was still for the best.

And he wondered if they might not be the ones who were right, after all—and the Letter wrong.

He would have liked to step to the door and hail some of those who were passing by so he could talk with them, but there was no one in the Ship (not even Mary) he could talk to.

Unless it were Joshua.

He sat eating, thinking of Joshua in the hydroponic gardens, pottering around, fussing with his plants.

As a boy, he'd gone there, along with the other boys, Joe and George and Herb and all the rest of them, Joshua then had been a man of middle age who always had a story and some sage advice and a smuggled tomato or a radish for a hungry boy. He had, Jon remembered, a soft gentle way of talking, and his eyes were honest eyes, and there was a gruff but winning friendliness about him.

It had been a long time, he realized, since he'd seen Joshua. Guilt, perhaps, he told himself.

But Joshua would be one who could understand the guilt. For once before he had understood.

It had been he and Joe, Jon remembered, who had sneaked in and stolen the tomatoes and been caught and lectured by the gardener. Joe and he had been friends ever since they had been toddlers. They had always been together. When there was devilment afoot the two of them were sure, somehow, to be in the middle of it.

Maybe Joe ... Jon shook his head. Not Joe, he thought. Even if he was his best friend, even if they had been pals as boys, even if they had stood up for each other when they had been married, even if they had been chess partners for more than twenty years— even so, Joe was not one he could tell about this thing.

"You still are thinking, dear," said Mary.

"I'll quit," said Jon. "Tell me about your day."

She told him. What Louise had said; and what Jane had said; and how foolish Molly was. The wild rumor and the terror and the slow quieting of the terror with the realization that, whatever came, it was for the best.

"Our Belief," she said, "is a comfort, Jon, at a time like this."

"Yes," said Jon. "A great comfort, indeed."

She got up from the bed. "I'm going down to see Louise," she said. "You'll stay here?" She bent and kissed him.

"I'll walk around until meeting time," he said.

He finished his meal, drank the water slowly, savoring each drop, then went out.

He headed for the hydroponic gardens. Joshua was there, a little older, his hair a little whiter, his shuffle more pronounced, but with the same kind crinkle about his eyes, the same slow smile upon his face.

And his greeting was the joke of old: "You come to steal tomatoes?"

"Not this time," said Jon.

"You and the other one."

"His name is Joe."

"I remember now. Sometimes I forget. I am getting older and sometimes I forget." His smile was quiet. "I won't take too long, lad. I won't make you and Mary wait."

"That's not so important now," said Jon.

"I was afraid that after what had happened you would not come to see me."

"It is the law," said Jon. "Neither you nor I, nor Mary, had anything to do with it. The law is right. We cannot change the law."

Joshua put out a hand and laid it on Jon's arm. "Look at the new tomatoes," he said. "They're the best I've ever grown. Just ready to be picked." He picked one, the ripest and the reddest, and handed it to Jon.

Jon rubbed the bright red fruit between his hands, feeling the smooth, warm texture of it, feeling the juice of it flow beneath the skin.

"They taste better right off the vine. Go ahead and eat it."

Jon lifted it to his mouth and set his teeth into it and caught the taste of it, the freshly picked taste, felt the soft pulp sliding down his throat.

"You were saying something, lad."

Jon shook his head.

"You have not been to see me since it happened," said Joshua. "The guilt of knowing I must die before you have a child kept you away from me. It's a hard thing, I grant—harder for you than it is for me. You would not have come except for a matter of importance."

Jon did not answer.

"Tonight," said Joshua, "you remembered you could talk to me. You used to come and talk with me often, because you remembered the talk you had with me when you were a kid."

"I broke the law," said Jon. "I came to steal tomatoes. Joe and I, and you caught us."

"I broke the law just now," said Joshua. "I gave you a tomato. It was not mine to give. It was not yours to take. But I broke the law because the law is nothing more than reason and the giving of one tomato does not harm the reason. There must be reason behind each law or there is no occasion for the law. If there is no reason, then the law is wrong."

"But to break a law is wrong."

"Listen," said Joshua. "You remember this morning?"

"Of course I do."

"Look at those tracks—the metal tracks, set deep into the metal, running up the wall."

Jon looked and saw them.

"That wall," said Joshua, "was the floor until this morning."

"But the tanks! They . . ."

"Exactly," said Joshua. "That's exactly what I thought. That's the first thing I thought when I was thrown out of bed. My tanks, I thought. All my beautiful tanks. Hanging up there on the wall. Fastened to the floor and hanging on the wall. With the water spilling out of them. With the plants dumped out of them. With the chemicals all wasted. But it didn't happen that way."

He reached out and tapped Jon on the chest.

"It didn't happen that way—not because of a certain law, but because of a certain reason. Look at the floor beneath your feet."

Jon looked down and the tracks were there, a continuation of the tracks that ran up the wall.

"The tanks are anchored to those tracks," said Joshua. "There are wheels enclosed within those tracks. When the floor changed to the wall, the tanks ran down the tracks and up the wall that became the floor and everything was all right. There was a little water spilled and some plants were damaged, but not many of them."

"It was planned," said Jon. "The Ship . . ."

"There must be reason to justify each law," Joshua told him. "There was reason here and a law as well. But the law was only a reminder not to violate the reason. If there were only reason you might forget it, or you might defy it or you might say that it had become outdated. But the law supplies authority and you follow law where you might not follow reason.

"The law said that the tracks on the wall, the old wall, that is, must be kept clear of obstacles and must be lubricated. At times we wondered why, for it seemed a useless law. But because it was a law we followed it quite blindly and so, when the Mutter came, the tracks were clear and oiled and the tanks ran up them. There was nothing in the way of their doing so, as there might have been if we'd not followed the law. For by following the law, we also followed the reason and it's the reason and not the law that counts."

"You're trying to tell me something," Jon said.

"I'm trying to tell you that we must follow each law blindly until we know the reason for it. And when we know, if we ever know, the reason and the purpose, we must then be able to judge whether the reason or the purpose is a worthy one. We must have the courage to say that it is bad, if it is bad. For if the reason is bad, then the law itself is bad, for a law is no more than a rule designed for a certain reason or to carry out a purpose."

"Purpose?"

"Certainly, lad, the purpose. For there must be some purpose. Nothing so well planned as the Ship could be without a purpose."

"The Ship itself? You think the Ship has purpose? They say . . ."

"I know what they say. Everything that happens must be for the best." He wagged his head. "There must have been a purpose, even for the Ship. Sometime, long ago, that purpose must have been plain and clear. But we've forgotten it. There must be certain facts and knowledge . . ."

"There was knowledge in the books," said Jon. "But they burned the books."

"There were certain untruths in them," said the old man. "Or what appeared to be untruths. But you cannot judge the truth until you have the facts, and I doubt they had the facts. There were other reasons, other factors.

"I'm a lonely man. I have a job to do, and not many come to visit. I have not had gossip to distract me although the Ship is full of gossip. I have thought. I have done a lot of thinking. I thought about us and the Ship. I thought about the laws and the purpose of it all.

"I have wondered what makes a plant grow, why water and chemicals are necessary to its growth. I have wondered why we must turn on the lamps for just so many hours—what is there in the lamps that helps a plant to grow? But if you forget to turn them on, the plant will start to die, so I know the lamps are needed, that the plants need, not water and chemicals alone, but the lamps as well.

"I have wondered why a tomato always grows on a tomato vine and why a cucumber always grows on a cucumber vine. You never find a tomato on a cucumber vine and there must be a reason.

"Behind even so simple a thing as the growing of tomatoes there must be a mass of reasons, certain basic facts. And we do not know these facts. We do not have the knowledge.

"I have wondered what it is that makes the lamps light up when you throw the switch.

"I have wondered what our bodies do with food. How does your body use that tomato you've just eaten? Why must we eat to live? Why must we sleep? How did we learn to talk?"

"I have never thought of all that," said Jon.

"You have never thought at all," said Joshua, "or almost not at all."

"No one does," said Jon.

"That is the trouble with the Ship," the old man told him. "No one ever thinks. They while away their time. They never dig for reasons. They never even wonder. Whatever happens must be for the best, and that's enough for them."

"I have just begun to think," said Jon.

"There was something you wanted," said the old man. "Some reason that you came."

"It doesn't matter now," said Jon. "You have answered it."

He went back, through the alleyways between the tanks, smelling the scent of green things growing, listening to the gurgle of the water running through the pumps. Back up the long corridors, with the stars shining true and steady now through the ports in the observation blisters.

Reason, Joshua had said. There is reason and a purpose. And that had been what the Letter had said, too—reason and a purpose. And as well as truths there will be untruths, and one must have certain knowledge to judge a thing, to say if it is true or not.

He squared his shoulders and went on.

The meeting was well under way when he reached the chapel, and he slid in quietly through the door and found Mary there. He stood beside her, and she slipped her hand in his and smiled. "You are late," she whispered.

"Sorry," he whispered back, and then they stood there, side by side, holding hands, watching the flicker of the two great candles that flanked the massive Holy Picture. Jon thought that never before had he seen it to such good advantage nor seen it quite so well, and he knew that it was a great occasion when they burned the candles for it.

He identified the men who sat below the Picture—Joe, his friend, and Greg and Frank. And he was proud that Joe, his friend, should be one of the three who sat beneath the Picture, for you must be pious and a leader to sit beneath the Picture.

They had finished reciting the Beginning and now Joe got up and began to lead them in the Ending.

"We go toward an End. There will be certain signs that shall foretell the coming of the End, but of the End itself no one may know, for it is unrevealed . . ."

Jon felt Mary's hand tighten upon his and he returned the pressure, and in the press of hand to hand he felt the comfort of a wife and of Belief and the security of the brotherhood of all the Folk.

It was a comfort, Mary had said while he had eaten the meal she had saved for him. There is comfort in our Belief, she'd said. And what she had said was true. There was comfort in Belief, comfort in knowing that it all was planned, that it was for the best, that even in the End it would be for the best.

They needed comfort, he thought. They needed comfort more than anything. They were so alone, especially so alone since the stars had stopped their spinning and stood still, since you could stand at a port and look out into the emptiness that lay between the stars. Made more alone by the lack of purpose, by the lack of knowing, although it was a comfort to know that all was for the best.

"The Mutter will come and the stars will stop their spin and they will stand naked and alone and bright in the depth of darkness, of the eternal darkness that covers everything except the Folk within the Ship. . . ."

And that was it, thought Jon. The special dispensation that gave them the comfort. The special knowing that they, of all the things there were, were sheltered and protected from eternal night.

Although, he wondered, how did the special knowing come about? From what source of knowledge did it spring? From what revelation? And blamed himself for thinking as he did, for it was not seemly that he should think such things at meeting in the chapel.

He was like Joshua, he told himself. He questioned everything. He wondered about the things that he had accepted all his life, that had been accepted without question for all the generations.

He lifted his head and looked at the Holy Picture—at the Tree and the Flowers and the River and the House far off, with the Sky that had Clouds in it and Wind you could not see but knew was there.

It was a pretty thing—it was beautiful. There were colors in it he had never seen anywhere except in the Pictures. Was there a place like that? Or was it only symbolism, only an idealization of the finest that was in the Folk, a distillation of the dreams of those shut up within the Ship?

Shut up in the Ship! He gasped that he had thought it. Shut up! Not shut up. Protected, rather. Protected and sheltered and kept from harm, set apart from all else which lay in the shadow of eternal night.

He bent his head in prayer, a prayer of contriteness and self-accusation. *Shut up!* That he should think a thing like that!

He felt Mary's hand in his and thought of the child they would have when Joshua was dead. He thought of the chess games he had played with Joe. He thought of the long nights in the darkness with Mary at his side.

He thought of his father, and the long-dead words thundered in his brain. And the Letter that spoke of knowledge and of destination and had a word of purpose.

What am I to do? he asked himself. Which road am I to follow? What is the Meaning and the End?

He counted the doors and found the right one and went in. The place was thick with dust, but the light bulb still survived. Against the farther wall was the door that was mentioned in the instruction sheet enclosed within the Letter—the door with the dial built into its center. A vault, the instruction sheet had said.

He walked across the floor, leaving footprints behind him in the dust, and knelt before the door. With his shirtsleeve he wiped the dust from the lock and read the numbers there. He laid the sheet upon the floor and grasped the dial. Turn the indicator first to 6, then to 15, back to 8, then to 22 and finally to 3.

He did it carefully, following the instructions, and at the final turn to 3 he heard the faint chucking sound of steel tumblers dropping into place.

He grasped the handle of the door and tugged, and the door came open slowly, because it was heavy.

He went inside and thumbed the switch and the lights came on, and everything was exactly as the instruction sheet had said. There was the bed and the machine beside it and the great steel box standing in one corner.

The air was foul, but there was no dust, since the vault was not tied in with the air-conditioning system which through centuries had spread the dust through all the other rooms.

Standing there alone, in the glare of the bulb, with the bed and machine and great steel box before him, terror came upon him, a ravening terror that shook him even as he tried to stand erect and taut to keep it away from him—a swift backlash of fear garnered from the many generations of unknowing and uncaring.

Knowledge—and there was a fear of knowledge, for knowledge was an evil thing. Years ago they had decided that, the ones who made decisions for the Ship, and they had made a law against Reading, and they had burned the books.

The Letter said that knowledge was a necessary thing.

And Joshua, standing beside the tomato tank, with the other tanks and their growing things about him, had said that there must be reason, and that knowledge would disclose the reason.

But it was only the Letter and Joshua—only the two of them against all the others, only the two of them against the decision that had been made many generations back.

No, he said, talking to himself, no, not those two alone—but my father and his father before him and fathers before that, handing down the Letter and the Book and the art of Reading. And he, himself, he knew, if he had had a child, would have handed him the Letter and the Book and would have taught him how to read. He could envision it—the two of them crouched in some obscure hiding place beneath the dim glow of a bulb, slowly studying out the way that letters went together to form the words, doing a thing that was forbidden, continuing a chain of heresy that had snaked its way throughout the Folk for many generations.

And here, finally, was the end result, the bed and machine and the great steel box. Here, at last, was the thing to which it all had pointed.

He went to the bed, approaching it gingerly, as if it might be a hidden trap. He poked and prodded it, and it was a bed and nothing more.

Turning from the bed to the machine, he went over it carefully, checking the wiring contacts as the instructions said he should, finding the cap, finding the switches, checking on other vital points. He found two loose contact points and tightened them, and finally, after some hesitation, he threw on the first switch, as the instructions said he should, and the red light glowed.

So he was all ready.

He climbed into the bed and took up the cap and set it on his head, twisting it securely into place.

Then he lay down and reached out and snapped on the second switch and there was a lullaby.

A lullaby, a singing, a tune running in his brain, and a sense of gentle rocking and of drowsiness.

* * * *

Jon Hoff went to sleep.

He woke and there was knowledge.

A slow, painful groping to recognize the place, the wall without the Holy Picture, the strange machine, the strange thick door, the cap upon his head.

His hands went up and took off the cap, and he held it, staring at it, and slowly he knew what it was.

Bit by painful bit, it all came back to him, the finding of the room, the opening of the vault, checking the machine and lying down with the cap tight upon his head.

The knowledge of where he was and why he was there—and a greater knowledge. A knowing of things he had not known before. Of frightening things.

He dropped the cap into his lap and sat stark upright, with his hands reaching out to grasp the edges of the bed.

Space! An emptiness. A mighty emptiness, filled with flaming suns that were called the stars. And across that space, across the stretches of it too vast to be measured by the mile, too great to be measured by anything but light-years, the space crossed by light in the passage of a year, sped a thing that was called a ship—not the Ship, Ship with a capital S, but simply a ship, one of many ships.

A ship from the planet Earth—not from the sun itself, not from the star, but from one of many planets that circled round the star.

It can't be, he told himself. It simply cannot be. The Ship can't move. There can't be space. There can't be emptiness. We can't be a single dot, a lost and wandering mote in the immensity of a universal emptiness, dwarfed by the stars that shine outside the port.

Because if that were so, then they stood for nothing. They were just casual factors in the universe.

Even less than casual factors. Less than nothing. A smear of wandering, random life lost amid the countless stars.

He swung his legs off the bed and sat there, staring at the machine.

Knowledge stored in there, he thought. That's what the instruction sheet had said. Knowledge stored on spools of tape, knowledge that was drummed into the brain, that was impressed, implanted, grafted on the brain of a sleeping man.

And this was just the beginning. This was only the first lesson. This was just the start of the old dead knowledge scrapped so long ago, a knowledge stored against a day of need, a knowledge hid away. And it was his. It lay upon the spools, it lay within the cap. It was his to take and his to use—and to what purpose? For there was no need to have the knowledge if there were no purpose in it.

And was it true? That was the question. Was the knowledge true? How could you know a truth? How could you recognize an untruth?

There was no way to know, of course—not yet was there a way to know the truth. Knowledge could be judged by other knowledge, and he had but little knowledge—more than anyone within the ship had had for years, yet still so little knowledge. For somewhere, he knew, there must be an explanation for the stars and for the planets that circled around the stars and for the space in which the stars were placed—and for the Ship that sped between the stars.

The Letter had said purpose and it had said destination and those were the two things he must know—the purpose and the destination.

He put the cap back in its place and went out of the vault and locked the door behind him, and he walked with a slightly surer stride, but still with the sense of guilt riding on his shoulders. For now he had broken not only the spirit, but the letter of the law—he was breaking the law for a reason, and he suspected that the reason and the purpose would wipe out the law.

He went down the long flights of the escalator stairs to the lower levels. He found Joe in the lounge, staring at the chess board with the pieces set and ready.

"Where have you been?" asked Joe. "I've been waiting for you."

"Just around," said Jon.

"This is three days," said Joe, "you've been just around." He looked at Jon quizzically, then continued. "Remember the hell we used to raise? The stealing and the tricks?"

"I remember, Joe."

"You always got a funny look about you just before we went off on one of our pranks. You have that same look now."

"I'm not up to any pranks," said Jon. "I'm not stealing anything."

"We've been friends for years," said Joe. "You've got something on your mind. . . ."

Looking down at him, Jon tried to see the boy, but the boy was gone. Instead was the man who sat beneath the Picture, the man who read the Ending, the pious man, the good man, a leader of the Ship's community.

He shook his head. "I'm sorry, Joe."

"I only want to help."

But if he knew, thought Jon, he wouldn't want to help. He'd look at me in horror, he'd report me to the chapel, he'd be the first to cry heresy. For it was heresy, there was no doubt of that. It was a denial of the Myth, it was a ripping away of the security of ignorance, it was a refutation of the belief that all would be for the best, it was saying they could no longer sit with folded hands and rely upon the planned order of the Ship.

"Let's play a game," he said with resolve.

"That's the way you want it, Jon?" demanded Joe.

"That's the way I want it."

"Your move," said Joe.

Jon moved his queen pawn. Joe stared at him. "You play a king's pawn game."

"I changed my mind," said Jon. "I think this opening's better."

"As you wish," said Joe.

They played. Joe won without any trouble.

At last, after days of lying on the bed and wearing the cap, of being lullabied to sleep and waking with new knowledge, Jon knew the entire story.

He knew about the Earth and how Earthmen had built the ship and sent it out to reach the stars, and he understood a little about the reaching for the stars that had driven humans to plan the ship.

He knew about the selection and the training of the crew, and the careful screening that had gone into the picking of the ancestors of the colonists-to-be, the biological recommendations that had determined their mating so that when the fortieth generation should finally reach the stars they would be a hardy race, efficient and ready to deal with the problems there.

He knew about the educational setup and the books that had been intended to keep knowledge intact, and he had some slight acquaintance with the psychology involved in the entire project.

But something had gone wrong. Not with the ship, but with the people in it.

The books had been fed into the converter. The Myth had risen and Earth had been forgotten. The knowledge had been lost and legend had been substituted. In the span of forty generations, the plan had been lost and the purpose been forgotten and the Folk lived out their lives in the sure and sane belief that they were self-contained, that the Ship was the beginning and the end, that by some divine intervention the Ship and the people in it had come into being, and that their ordered lives were directed by a worked-out plan in which everything that happened must be for the best.

They played chess and cards and listened to old music, never questioning for a moment who had invented cards or chess or who had created music. They whiled away not hours, but lives, with long gossiping, and told old stories, and swapped old yarns out of other generations. But they had no history and they did not wonder and they did not look ahead—for everything that happened would be for the best.

For year on empty year the Ship was all they had known. Even before the first generation had died, the Earth had become a misty thing far behind, not only in time and space, but in memory as well. There was no loyalty to Earth to keep alive the memory of the Earth. There was no loyalty to the Ship, because the Ship had no need of it.

The Ship was a mother to them, and they nestled in it. The Ship fed them and sheltered them and kept them safe from harm.

There was no place to go. Nothing to do. Nothing to think about. And they adapted.

Babies, Jon Hoff thought. Babies cuddling in a mother's arms. Babies prattling old storied rhymes on the nursery floor. And some of the rhymes were truer than they knew.

It had been spoken that when the Mutter came and the stars stood still the End was near at hand.

And that was true enough, for the stars had moved because the Ship was spuming on its longitudinal axis to afford artificial gravity. But when the Ship neared the destination, it would automatically halt the spin and resume its normal flight, with things called gyroscopes taking over to provide the gravity.

Even now the Ship was plunging down toward the star and the solar system at which it had been aimed. Plunging down upon it if—and Jon Hoff sweated as he thought of it—if it had not already overshot its mark.

For the people might have changed, but the Ship did not. The Ship did not adapt. The Ship remembered when its passengers forgot. True to the taped instructions that had been fed into it more than a thousand years before, it had held its course, it had retained the purpose, it had kept its rendezvous, and even now it neared its destination.

Automatic, but not entirely automatic. It could not establish an orbit around the target planet without the help of a human brain, without a human hand to tell it what to do. For a thousand years it might get along without its human, but in the final moment it would need a man to complete its purpose.

And I, Jon Hoff told himself, *I* am that man.

Yet he was only one man. Could one man alone do it?

He thought about the others. About Joe and Herb and George and all the rest of them, and there was none of them that he could trust, no one of them to whom he could go and tell what he had done.

He held the Ship within his mind. He knew the theory and the operation, but it might take more than theory and more than operation. It might take familiarity and training. A man might have to live with a ship before he could run it. And there'd be no time for him to live with it.

He stood beside the machine that had given him the knowledge, with all the tape run through it now, with its purpose finally accomplished, as the Letter had accomplished its purpose, as Mankind and the Ship would accomplish theirs if his brain was clear and his hand was steady. And if he knew enough.

There was yet the chest standing in the corner. He would open that—and finally it would be done. All that those others could do for him would then be done and the rest would depend on him.

Moving slowly, he knelt before the chest and opened the lid.

There were rolls of paper, many rolls of it, and beneath the paper, books, dozens of books, and in one corner a glassite capsule enclosing a piece of mechanism that he knew could be nothing but a gun, although he'd never seen one.

He reached for the glassite capsule and lifted it, and beneath the capsule was an envelope with one word printed on it: KEYS.

He took the envelope and tore it open and there were two keys. The tag on one said: CONTROL ROOM; the tag on the other: ENGINE ROOM.

He put the keys in his pocket and grasped the glassite capsule. With a quick twitch, he wrenched it in two. There was a little puffing sound as the vacuum within the tube puffed out, and the gun lay in his hands.

It was not heavy, but heavy enough to give it authority. It had a look of strength about it and a look of grim cruelty, and he grasped it by the butt and lifted it and pointed, and he felt the ancient surge of vicious power—the power of Man, the killer—and he was ashamed.

He laid the gun back in the chest and drew out one of the rolls of paper. It crackled, protesting, as he gently unrolled it. It was a drawing of some sort, and he bent above it to make out what it was, worrying out the printed words.

He couldn't make head or tail of it, so he put it down and it rolled into a cylinder again as if it were alive.

He took out another one and unrolled it, and this time it was a plan for a section of the Ship.

Another one and another one, and they were sections of the Ship, too—the corridors and escalators, the observation blisters, the cubicles.

And finally he unrolled one that showed the Ship itself, a cross-section of it, with all the cubicles in place and the hydroponic gardens. And up in the nose the control room, and in the back the engine rooms.

He spread it out and studied it and it wasn't right, until he figured out that if you cut off the control room and the engine room it would be. And that, he told himself, was the way it should be, for someone long ago had locked both control and engine rooms to keep them safe from harm—to keep them safe from harm against this very day.

To the Folk, the engine room and control room had simply not existed, and that was why, he told himself, the blueprint had seemed wrong.

He let the blueprint roll up unaided and took out another one, and this time it was the engine room. He studied it, crinkling his brow, trying to make out what was there, and while there were certain installations he could guess at, there were many that he couldn't.

He made out the converter and wondered how the converter could be in a locked engine room when they'd used it all these years. But finally he saw that the converter had two openings, one beyond the hydroponic gardens and the other within the engine room itself.

He let go of the blueprint and it rolled up, just like all the others. He crouched there, rocking on his toes a little, staring at the blueprints, thinking: If there were any further proof needed to convince me, there lies that simple proof.

Plans and blueprints for the ship. Plans dreamed by men and drawn by human hands. A dream of stars drawn on a piece of paper. No divine intervention. No myth. Just simple human planning.

He thought of the Holy Pictures, and he wondered what they were. They, too—could they, too, be as wide of the mark as the story of the Myth? And if they were, it seemed a shame. For they were such a comfort. And the Belief as well. It had been a comfort, too.

He crouched in the smallness of the vault, with the machine and bed and chest, with the rolled-up blueprints at his feet, and brought up his arms across his chest and hugged himself in what was almost abject pity.

He wished that he had never started. He wished there had been no Letter. He wished that he were back again, in the ignorance and security. Back again, playing chess with Joe.

Joe said, from the doorway, "So this is where you've been hiding out."

He saw Joe's feet, planted on the floor, and he let his eyes move up, following Joe's body until he reached his face. The smile was frozen there. A half-smiled smile frozen solid on Joe's face.

"Books!" said Joe.

It was an obscene word. The way Joe said it, it was an obscene word. As if one had been caught in some unmentionable act, surprised with a dirty thought dangling naked in one's mind.

"Joe—" said Jon.

"You wouldn't tell me," said Joe. "You said you didn't want my help. I don't wonder that you didn't . . ."

"Joe, listen—"

"Sneaking off with books," said Joe.

"Look, Joe. Everything's all wrong. People like us made this ship. It is going somewhere. I know the meaning of the End . . ."

The wonder and the horror were gone from Joe's face now. It had become bleak. It was a judge's face.

It towered above him and there was no mercy in it—not even any pity.

"Joe!"

Joe turned around swiftly, leaping for the door.

"Joe! Wait a minute, Joe!" But he was gone.

The sound of his feet came back, the sound of them running along the corridor, heading for the escalator that would take him down to the living levels.

Running back and going down to cry up the pack. To send them tonguing through the entire ship, hunting down Jon Hoff. And when they caught Jon Hoff . . .

When they caught Jon Hoff, that would be the End for always. That would make the End the kind of unknown End that was spoken in the chapel. For there would be no other—there would never be another who would know the Meaning and the Purpose and the Destination.

And because of that, thousands of men and women would have died in vain. The sweat and genius and longing of the people who had launched the ship would have been for nothing.

It would be a terrible waste. And wasting was a crime. You must not waste. You must not throw away. And that meant human lives and dreams as well as food and water.

Jon's hand reached out and grasped the gun, and his fingers tightened on it as the rage grew in him, the rage of desperation, the last-hope rage, the momentary, almost blinded madness of a man who sees the rug of life being deliberately jerked from beneath his feet.

Although it was not his life alone, but the lives of all the others—Mary's life, and Herb's, and Louise's and Joshua's as well.

He was running at full tilt when he went out the door, and he skidded as he made the sharp right-angle turn into the corridor. He flung himself in the direction of the escalator, and in the darkness felt the treads beneath his feet, and he breathed a thankfulness for the many times he had gone from the living quarters to the center of the Ship, feeling his way in darkness. For now he was at home in the darkness, and that was an advantage he had that Joe did not possess.

He hurled himself down the stairs, skidded, and raced along

the corridor, found the second flight—and ahead of him he heard the running, stumbling footsteps of the man who fled ahead of him.

In the next corridor, he knew, there was a single lamp, burning dimly at the end of the corridor. If he could reach the corridor in time . . .

He went down the treads, one hand on the rail to keep himself from falling, scarcely touching the metal, sliding down rather than running.

He hit the floor in a crouch, bent low, and there, outlined against the dimly burning lamp, was a running figure. He lifted the gun and pressed the button, and the gun leaped in his hands and the corridor suddenly was filled with flame.

The light blinded him for a second, and he remained in a crouch there, and the thought ran through him: *I've killed Joe, my friend.*

Except it wasn't Joe. It wasn't the boy he'd grown up with. It wasn't the man who had sat opposite him at the chess board. It was not Joe, his friend. It was someone else—a man with a judge's face, a man who had run to cry up the pack, a man who would have condemned them all to the End that was unknown.

He felt somehow that he was right, but nevertheless he trembled.

His sight came back and there was a huddled blackness on the floor. And now his hand was shaking and he crouched there without moving and felt the sickness heaving at his stomach and the weakness crawl along his body.

You must not waste.

You must not throw away.

Those were spoken laws. But there were other laws that never had been spoken because there had been no need to speak them. They had not spoken *you must not steal another's wife*, they had not spoken *you must not bear false witness*, they had not spoken *you must not kill*—for those were crimes that had been wiped out long before the starship had leaped away from Earth.

Those were the laws of decency and good taste. And he had broken one of them. He had killed a fellow man. He had killed his friend.

Except, he told himself, he was not my friend. He was an enemy—the enemy of all of us.

Jon Hoff stood erect and stopped his body's shaking. He thrust the gun into his belt and walked woodenly down the corridor toward the huddle on the floor. The darkness made it a little easier, for he could not see what lay there as well as if it had been light.

The face lay against the floor and he could not see the face. It would have been harder had the face stared up at him.

He stood there considering. In just a little while, the Folk would miss Joe and would start to hunt for him. And they must not find him. They must never know. The idea of killing had long since been wiped away; there could be no suggestion of it. For if one man killed, no matter how or why, then there might be others who would kill. If one man sinned, his sinning must be hidden, for from one sinning might come other sinning, and when they reached the new world, when (and if) they reached the target planet, they would need all the inner strength, all the fellowship and fellow-security they could muster up.

He could not hide the body, for there was no hiding place but could be found. He could not feed it to the converter because he could not reach the converter. To reach it, he'd have to go through the hydroponic gardens.

But no, of course he wouldn't. There was another way to reach the converter—through the engine room.

He patted his pocket and the keys were there. He bent and grasped Joe and recoiled at the touch of the flesh, still warm. He shrank back against the metal wall and stood there, and his stomach churned, and the guilt of what he'd done hammered in his head.

He thought of his father talking to him—the granite-faced old man—and he thought of the man who had written the Letter, and he thought of all the others who had passed it on, committing heresy for the sake of truth, for the sake of knowledge and salvation.

There had been too much ventured, too much dared and braved, too many lonely nights of wondering if what one did was right, to lose it now because of squeamishness or guilt.

He walked out from the wall and grasped the body and slung it on his shoulder.

It dangled. It gurgled. Something wet and warm trickled down his back.

He gritted his teeth to keep them from chattering. And he staggered along beneath his burden, climbing the long-stilled escalators, clopping along the corridors, heading for the engine room.

At last he reached the door and laid the burden down to fumble for the keys. He found them and selected the right one and turned it in the door, and when he pushed against the door, it swung slowly open. A gust of warm air came out and slapped him in the face. Lights glowed brightly, and there was a humming song of power and the whine of spinning metal.

He reached down and lifted Joe again and went in and closed the door. He stood staring down the long paths that ran between the great machines.

There was one machine that spun, and he recognized it—a gyroscope, a stabilizer hanging in its gimbals, humming to itself.

How long would it take a man to understand all there was to know about all these massive, intricate machines? How far have we fallen from the knowledge of a thousand years ago?

And the thing he carried dangled on his shoulder, and he heard the slow, deliberate dripping of the warm, sticky liquid splashing on the floor.

Horror and wonder—a going back. A going back through a thousand years to a knowledge that could build machines like these. A going back much farther to an instability of human emotions that would drive one man to kill another man.

I must be rid of him, Jon Hoff thought bitterly. *I must be rid of him. But I never will be. When he has disappeared, when he has become something other than what he is, when the substances of him have become something else, I still shall not be rid of him. Never!*

He found the converter door and braced himself in front of it. He tugged at the door. It stuck, and he jerked at it, and it came free. The maw gaped, large enough to take a human body, and from behind the baffles he could hear the roaring of the power and imagined that he caught the hellish flicker of the ravening fire. He balanced the body on his shoulder and slid it off as gently as he could, feeding it to the maw. He gave it a final push and closed the door and trod hard upon the feeder mechanism.

The deed finally was done.

He reeled back from the converter's face and mopped his brow. Now the burden was gone, but it still was with him. As it always would be, he thought. As it always would be.

The footsteps came at him, and he did not swing around to face them, for he knew whose the footsteps were—the ghostly footsteps that would dog him all his life—the footsteps of guilt walking in his mind.

A voice said, "Lad, what have you done?"

Jon said, "I have killed a man. I have killed my friend." And he swung around to face the footsteps and the voice, because neither was a ghost.

Joshua said, "There was a reason for it, lad?"

"A reason," said Jon Hoff. "A reason and a purpose."

"You need a friend," Joshua said. "You need a friend, my boy."

Jon nodded. "I found the purpose of the Ship. And the destination. He found me out. He was going to denounce me. I—I—"

"You killed him."

"I thought, *One life or all?* I took only one life. He would have taken all."

They stood for a long moment, facing each other.

The old man said, "It is not right to take a life. It is not right nor proper."

He stood there, stumpy and stolid, against the background of the engines, but there was something vital in him, some driving force within him as there was in the engines.

"Nor is it right," he said, "to condemn the Folk to a fate that was not intended. It is not right to let a purpose go by default and ignorance." After a pause, he asked. "The purpose of the Ship? It is a good purpose?"

"I do not know," said Jon. "I can't be sure. But at least it is a purpose. A purpose, any purpose, is better than none at all." He raised his head and brushed back his hair, plastered down with sweat across his brow.

"All right," he said. "I'll go along with you. I've taken one life. I'll not take any more."

Joshua spoke slowly, gently. "No, lad. I am the one who goes along with you."

To see the great depth of the emptiness in which the stars blazed like tiny, eternal watch fires was bad enough when one looked out a blister port. To see it from the control room, where the great glass plate opened out into the very jaws of space, was something else again.

You could look down and down and there was no bottom, and you could look up or out and there was no stopping, and one moment you would swear that a certain star could be reached for and plucked, and the next moment it was so far away that your brain spun with the very thought of distance.

The stars were far.

All but one of them. And that one blazed, a flaming sun, off toward the left.

Jon Hoff flicked a glance at Joshua, and the old man's face was frozen in a mask that was disbelief and fear and something touching horror.

And, he thought, I knew. I knew what it might be like. I had some idea. But he had none at all.

He pulled his eyes from the vision plate and saw the banks of instruments, and his stomach seemed to turn over and his fingers were all thumbs. No time to get to know it as it really is. What must be done, he must do by intellect alone, by the sketchy knowledge impressed upon his brain—a brain that was not trained or ready, that would not be trained and ready for many years.

"What are we to do?" Joshua whispered. "Lad, what are we to do?"

And Jon Hoff thought: What *are* we to do?

He walked slowly forward and mounted the steps to the chair that said NAVIGATOR on the back of it.

Slowly he hoisted himself into the chair, and it seemed that he sat on the edge of space itself, that he sat upon a precipice from which at any moment he might slip off and tumble into space.

He put his hands down carefully and gripped the chair's arms and hung on tight and fought to orient himself, to know that he sat in a navigator's chair and that in front of him were trips and buttons that he could press or trip, and that the pressing and the tripping of them would send signals to the pulsing engines.

"That star," said Joshua. "That big one off to the left. The burning one..."

"All the stars are burning."

"But that one. The big one..."

"That's the one we headed for a thousand years ago," said Jon. And he hoped it was. He wished he could be certain that it was the one.

Even as he thought it, bells of alarm were ringing in his brain. There was something wrong.

Something very wrong. He tried to think, but space was too close to think, space was, too big and empty and there was no use of thinking. One could not outwit space. One could not fight space. It was too big and cruel. Space did not care. It had no mercy in it. It did not care what happened to the ship or the people in it.

The only ones who had ever cared had been the people back on Earth who had launched the Ship, and, for a little while, the Folk who rode the Ship. And finally, he and one old man. They two against all space. The only ones who cared.

"It's bigger than the others," said Joshua. "We are closer to it."

That was what was wrong! That was what had rung the alarm within his mind. The star was far too close—it shouldn't be that close!

He wrenched his eyes from space and looked down at the control board, and all he saw was a meaningless mass of trips and levers, banks of buttons, rows of dials.

He watched the board, and slowly his mind began to sort it out, to make some sense of it, the knowledge the machine had pounded into him beginning to take over. He read the dials, and he got some knowledge from them. He located certain controls that he had to know about. Mathematics rose unbidden in his brain and did a nightmare dance.

It was useless. It had been a good idea, but it hadn't worked. You couldn't educate a man by a machine. You couldn't pound into him the knowledge necessary to navigate a ship.

"I can't do it, Joshua," he cried. "It's impossible to do it."

Where were the planets? How could he find the planets? And when he found them, if he found them, what would he do then?

The Ship was falling toward the sun.

He didn't know where to look for planets. And they were going too fast—they were going far too fast.

Sweat burst out upon him, beading his brow and running down his face, dripping from his armpits.

"Take it easy, lad. Take it easy now."

He tried to take it easy, but it didn't work. He reached down and slid open the tiny drawer beneath the control panel. There was paper there and pencils. He took out a sheet of paper and a pencil. He jotted down the readings on the dials: absolute velocity;

increase of velocity; distance from the star; angular approach to the star.

There were other readings, but those were the essential ones, those were the ones that counted.

And one thought rose in his brain, one thought that had been impressed upon it time after time: To navigate a ship is not a matter of driving it toward a certain point, but of knowing where it will be at any time within the immediate future.

He made his calculations, the mathematics struggling upward into his consciousness. He made the calculations, and he made a graph and then reached out and pushed a control lever forward two notches and hoped that he was right.

"You are making it out?" Joshua asked.

Jon shook his head. "We'll know—an hour from now we'll know."

A slight increase in thrust to keep the Ship from plunging too close toward the sun. Skirting the sun and curving back, under the attraction of the sun, making a long wide loop out into space, and then back toward the sun again. That was the way it worked—that was the way he hoped it worked. That was the way the machine had told him it might work.

He sat there limp, wondering about the strange machine. How much reliance could you put in tape running on a spool and a cap clamped on your head?

"We'll be here a long time," said Joshua.

Jon nodded. "I am afraid so, Joshua. It will take a long time."

"Then," the old man said, "I'll go and get some food." He started toward the door, then turned back.

"Mary?" he asked.

Jon shook his head. "Not yet. Let's leave them in peace. If we fail..."

"We won't fail." Jon spoke sharply. "If we do, it's best they never know."

"You may be right," the old man said. "I'll go and get the food."

Two hours later, Jon knew that the Ship would not crash the sun. It would come close, almost too close for comfort—only a million miles or so away—but the Ship's velocity would be such that it would skim past the sun and climb out into space again, pulled to one side by the attraction of the sun, fighting outward against the pull of the flaming star, dropping off its speed on the upward, outward haul.

With its flight path curved inward by the sun, it would establish an orbit—a highly dangerous orbit, for on the next swing around, left to its own devices, the ship would crash the sun.

Between the time that it passed the sun and curved inward once again, he must establish control over it, but the important thing was that he had bought some time. Without the added two notches of velocity he had gained by the shoving of the lever, he was sure, the ship either would have plunged into the sun or would have established a tightening orbit about it from which even the fantastic power of the mighty engines could not have pulled it free.

He had time, and he had some knowledge, and Joshua had gone to bring some food. He had time, and he had to use the time. He had the knowledge, lying somewhere in his brain, planted there, and he must dig it up and put it to the job for which it was intended.

He was calmer now and a little surer of himself. And he wondered, in his own awkwardness, how the men who had launched the ship from Earth, the men who had watched and tended it before the Ignorance, could have shot so closely. Chance, perhaps, for it would have been impossible to shoot a thousand-year-long missile at a tiny target and have it hold its course—or would it have been possible?

Automatic... automatic... automatic... The word thrummed in his brain. The single word over and over again. The ship was automatic. It ran itself, it repaired itself, it serviced itself, it held true to the target. It needed only the hand and brain of Man to tell it what to do. Do this, the hand and brain of Man would say, and the Ship would do it. That was all that was needed—the simple telling of instructions.

The problem was how to tell the Ship. What and how to tell it. And there were certain facts that haunted him about the telling of the Ship.

He got down from the navigator's chair and prowled about the room. There was a thin, fine dust on everything, but when he rubbed his sleeve along the metal, the metal shone as brightly as on that day it had been installed.

He found things, and some of them he knew and recognized

and some of them he didn't. But, most and after some trials and errors, he remembered how to operate it.

And now he knew how to find the planets—if this was the target star and there were any planets.

Three hours gone and Joshua had not returned. It was too long to be gone just to get some food. Jon paced up and down the room, fighting down his fears. Something had happened, something must have happened to the old man.

He went back to the telescope and began the work of running down the planets. It was hard work and purposeless at first, but bit by bit, with the handling of the instruments, the facts started drifting up into his consciousness.

He found one planet—and there was a knock upon the door. He left the telescope and strode across the room.

The corridor was full of people, and all at once they were shouting at him, shouting hateful words, and the roaring of their voices was a blast of anger and of condemnation that sent him back a step.

In front were Herb and George and behind them all the others—men and women both. He looked for Mary, but he didn't see her.

The crowd surged forward, and there was hatred and loathing on their faces, and the fog of fear came out of them and struck deep into Jon Hoff.

His hand went down to his waistband and closed upon the gun butt, and he dragged the weapon free.

He tilted the gun downward and stabbed at the button, just one quick, light stab. Light bloomed out and filled the doorway, and the crowd went reeling back. The door itself was blackened and there was the smell of blistered paint.

Jon Hoff spoke evenly.

"This is a gun," he said. "With it, I can kill you. I *will* kill you if you interfere. Stand back. Go back where you came."

Herb took a forward step and stopped. "You are the one who is interfering," he declared. He took another step.

Jon brought the gun up and lined its sights on him.

"I've killed one man," he said, "and I'll kill another." And he thought, *So easy to talk of killing, of taking human life. So ready to do it, now that I've killed once.*

"Joe is missing," said Herb. "We have been hunting for him."

"You need to hunt no more," said Jon.

"But Joe was your friend."

"And so are you," said Jon. "But the purpose is too big for friendship. You're with me or against me. There is no middle ground."

"We'll read you out of chapel."

"You'll read me out of chapel," said Jon, mocking him.

"We'll exile you to the central ship."

"We've been exiled all our lives," said Jon. "For many generations. And we didn't even know it. We didn't know, I tell you. And because we didn't know, we fixed up a pretty story. We fixed up a pretty story, and we convinced ourselves of it, and we lived by it. And when I come along and show you it was no more than a pretty story, dreamed up because we had to have a story—had to have, I say—you are ready to read me out of chapel and to exile me. You'll have to do better than that, Herb. Much better than that." He patted the gun. "I can do better than that," he said.

"Jon, you are mad."

"And you are a fool," said Jon.

At first he had been afraid, then he had been angry, and now there was only contempt—only contempt for them, huddled in the corridor, voicing feeble threats.

"What did you do with Joshua?" he asked.

"We tied him up," said Herb.

"Go back and untie him and send me up some food," he said.

They wavered. He made a threatening motion with the gun.

"Go," he said.

They ran.

He slammed the door and went back to the telescope.

He found six planets, and two had atmospheres, the second and fifth. He looked at his watch, and many hours had gone by. Joshua had still not appeared. There had been no rap at the door. There was no food and water. He climbed the steps to the navigator's chair again.

The star was far astern. The velocity had slid way off but was still too fast.

He pulled the lever back and watched the velocity indicator drop. It was safe to do that—he hoped it was safe to do it. The Ship was thirty million out, and it should be safe to cut velocity.

He studied the board, and it was clearer now, more understandable—there were more things he knew about. It was not so hard, he thought. It would not be too hard. You had time. You had plenty of time.

You had to plan ahead, but you had time to do it.

He studied the board, and he found the computator, the little metal brain—and that was how you told the Ship. That was what he had missed before—that was what he had wondered about— how to tell the Ship. And this was the way you told it. You told the little brain.

The one word—*automatic*—kept on hounding him. He found the stud that was labeled telescope and the one that was labeled orbit and still another that was labeled landing.

That was it, he thought. After all the worry, after all the fears, it was as simple as all that. For that would have been the way those back on Earth would have made the Ship. Simple. Simple beyond belief.

So simple that any fool could land it. Just anyone at all who could punch a button. For certainly they must have feared or guessed what might happen on the Ship after several generations. They must have known how Earth would be forgotten and that there would be a cultural adaptation to the Ship. Feared or guessed—or planned? Was the culture of the Ship a part of the master plan? Could the Folk have lived through a thousand years if they had known of the purpose and the destination?

And the answer seemed to be that they wouldn't have been able to, for they would have felt robbed and cheated, would have gone mad with the knowledge that they were no more than carriers of life, that their lives and the lives of many generations after them would be canceled out so that after many generations their descendants could arrive at the target planet.

There had been only one way to beat that situation—and that was to forget what it was all about. And that is what had happened, and it had been for the best.

The Folk, after the first few generations, had lived their little lives in the little circle of their home-grown culture, and that had been enough. After that, the thousand years had been as nothing, for no one knew about the thousand years.

And all the time the Ship bored on through space, heading for the target, heading straight and true.

Jon Hoff went down to the telescope and centered Planet V and clamped over the radar controls that would hold it centered. He went back to the computator and pushed the stud that said telescope and the other stud that said orbit.

Then he sat down to wait. There was nothing more to do.

Planet V was death.

The analyzer told the story. The atmosphere was mostly methane, the gravity thirty times too great, the pressure beneath the boiling clouds of methane close to a thousand atmospheres. There were other factors, too. But any one of those three would have been enough.

Jon Hoff pulled the Ship out of its orbit, headed it sunward. Back at the telescope, he found Planet II, locked it in the sights, tied in the computator and sat down to wait again.

One chance more, and that was all they had. For all of the planets, only two had atmospheres. It had to be Planet II or none.

And if the second planet turned out to be death as well, what then?

There was one answer. There could be no other. Head the Ship toward another star, build up velocity, and hope—hope that in another several generations the Folk could find a planet they could live on.

He was hungry—his belly gaunt and sore. He had found a water cooler with a few cups of liquid still intact, but he'd drunk the last of that two days before.

Joshua had not come back. There had been no sign from the Folk. Twice he had opened the door and gone out into the corridor, ready to make a dash for food and water, then had reconsidered and gone back in again. For he couldn't take the chance. He couldn't take the chance that they would sight him and run him down and not let him go back to the control room.

But the time would come before too long when he'd have to take a chance—when he'd have to make the dash. For before another day was gone, he might be too weak to make it. And there were many days ahead before they would reach Planet II.

The time would come when he'd have no choice. That he could stick it out was impossible. If he did not get food and water, he'd be a useless, crawling hulk with the strength and mind gone out of him by the time they reached the planet.

He went back to the control board and looked things over. It seemed to be all right. The Ship was still building up velocity. The monitor on the computator was clocking its blue light and chuckling to itself, saying, *Everything's all right, everything's all right.*

Then he went back down the steps and to the corner where he'd been sleeping. He lay down and curled himself into a ball, trying to squeeze his belly together so that it wouldn't nag him. He shut his eyes and tried to go to sleep.

With his ear against the metal, he could hear the pulsing of the engines far back in their room—the song of power that ran through all the Ship. And he remembered how he had thought a man might have to live with a ship to run her. But it hadn't turned out that way, although he could see how a man might learn to live with a ship, how a ship might become a part of him.

He dozed off and woke, then dozed again—and this time there was a voice shouting and someone hammering at the door.

He came to his feet in one lithe motion, scrambled for the door, the key already in his fist, stabbing at the lock. He jerked the door open, and Mary stumbled in. She carried a great square can in one hand, a huge sack in the other, and boiling down the corridor toward the door was a running mob that brandished clubs and screamed.

Jon reached down and hauled Mary clear, then slammed the door and locked it. He heard the running bodies thud against the door and then the clubs pounding at it and the people screaming.

Jon stooped above his wife. "Mary," he said, his voice choking and his throat constricting. "Mary."

"I had to come," she said, and she was crying when she said it. "I had to come, no matter what you did."

"What I have done," he said, "has been for the best. It was a part of the Plan, Mary. I am convinced of that. Part of the Master Plan. The people back on Earth had it all planned out. I just happened to be the one who—"

"You are a heretic," she said. "You've destroyed our Belief. You have set the Folk at one another's throat. You . . ."

"I know the truth," he said. "I know the purpose of the Ship."

She reached up her hands and cupped his face between her palms and pulled his head down and cuddled him.

"I don't care," she said. "I don't care. Not any more, I don't. I did at first. I was angry with you, Jon. I was ashamed of you. I almost died of shame. But when they killed Joshua . . ."

"What was that?"

"They killed Joshua. They beat him to death. And he's not the only one. There were others who wanted to come and help you. Just a few of them. They killed them, too. There's killing in the Ship. And hate. And suspicion. And all sorts of ugly rumors. It never was like that before. Not before you took away Belief."

A culture shattered, he thought. Shattered in the matter of an hour. A belief twitched away in the breadth of one split second. There was madness and killing. Of course there'd be.

"They are afraid," he said. "Their security is gone."

"I tried to come earlier," Mary said. "I knew you must be hungry, and I was afraid there'd be no water. But I had to wait until no one was watching."

He held her tight against him, and his eyes were a little dim.

"There's food," she said, "and water. I brought all that I could carry."

"My wife," he said. "My darling wife . . ."

"There's food, Jon. Why don't you eat?"

He rose and pulled her to her feet.

"In just a minute," he said, "I'll eat in just a minute. First, I want to show you something. I want to show you Truth."

He led her up the steps.

"Look out there," he said. "That is where we're going. This is where we've been. No matter what we might have told ourselves, that out there is Truth."

Planet II was the Holy Pictures come to life entire. There were Trees and Brooks, Flowers and Grass, Sky and Clouds, Wind and Sunshine.

After the Ship had landed, Mary and Jon stood beside the navigator's chair and stared out through the vision plate.

The analyzer gurgled slightly and spat out its report. *Safe for humans*, said the printed slip, adding a great deal of data about atmospheric composition, bacterial count, violet-ray intensity, and many other things. But the one conclusion was enough. *Safe for humans.*

Jon reached out his hand for the master switch in the center of the Board.

"This is it," he said. "This is the end of the thousand years."

He turned the switch, and the dials all clicked to zero. The needles found dead center. The song of power died out in the Ship, and there was the olden silence—the silence of long ago, of the time when the stars were streaks and the walls were floors.

Then they heard the sound—the sound of human wailing, as an animal might howl.

"They are afraid," said Mary. "They are scared to death. They won't leave the Ship."

And she was right. That was something that he had not thought of—that they would not leave the Ship. They had been tied to it for many generations. They had looked to it for shelter and security. To them, the vastness of the world outside, the never-ending Sky, the lack of a boundary of any sort at all, would be sodden terror.

Somehow or other they would have to be driven from the Ship—literally driven from it, and the Ship locked tight so they could not fight their way back in again. For the Ship was ignorance and cowering; it was a shell outgrown; it was the womb from which the race would be born anew.

Mary asked, "What will they do to us? I never thought of that. We can't hide from them, or . . ."

"Not anything," said Jon. "They won't do anything. Not while I have this." He slapped the gun at his side.

"But, Jon, this killing . . ."

"There won't be any killing. They will be afraid, and the fear will force them to do what must be done. After a time, maybe a long time, they will come to their senses, and then there will be no further fear. But to start with, there is a need of . . ."

The knowledge stirred within his brain, the knowledge implanted there by the strange machine.

"Leadership," he said. "That is what they'll need—someone to lead them, to tell them what to do, to help them to work together."

He thought bitterly, *I believed that it had ended, but it hasn't ended. Bringing down the Ship was not enough. I must go on from here. No matter what I do, as long as I live, there will be no end to it.*

There was the getting settled, and the learning once again. There were the books in the chest, more than half the chest packed full of books. Basic texts, perhaps. The books that would be needed for the starting over. And somewhere, too, instructions? Instructions left with the books for a man like him to read and carry out?

**INSTRUCTIONS TO BE PUT INTO EFFECT
AFTER LANDING**

That would be the notation the envelope would carry, or another very like it, and he'd tear the envelope open, and there would be folded pages. Once before, in another letter, there had been folded pages. And the second letter? There would be one, he was sure.

"It was planned on Earth," he said. "Every step was planned. They planned the great forgetting as the only way humans could carry out the flight. They planned the heresy that handed down the knowledge. They made the Ship so simple that anyone could handle it—anyone at all. They looked ahead and saw what was bound to happen. Their planning has been just a jump ahead of us every moment."

He stared out the vision plate at the sweep of land, at the Trees and Grass and Sky.

"I wouldn't be surprised," he said, "if they figured out how to drive us off the Ship."

A loud-speaker came to life and talked throughout the Ship, so that everyone might hear.

"*Now hear this,*" it said, the old recording just a little scratchy. "*Now hear this. You must leave the Ship within the next twelve hours. At the expiration of that time, a deadly gas will be released inside the Ship. Now hear this . . .*"

Jon reached out his hand to Mary. "I was right," he said. "They planned it to the last. They're still that jump ahead of us."

They stood there, the two of them, thinking of those people who had planned so well, who had thought so far ahead, who had known the problems and had planned against them.

"Come on," he said. "Let's go."

"Jon."

"Yes?"

"Can we have children now?"

"Yes," he said. "We can have children. Anyone who wishes may. On the Ship, there were so many of us. Now on this planet, there are so few of us."

"There is room," said Mary. "Room to spare."

He unlocked the control room door, carefully locked it behind him. They went down the darkened corridors.

The loud-speaker continued: *"Now hear this. Now hear this. You must leave the Ship . . ."*

Mary shrank against him, and he felt the trembling of her body.

"Jon. Are we going out now? Are we going out?"

Frightened. Of course, she was frightened. He was frightened, too. One does not slough off entirely the fears of generations, even in the light of truth.

"Not right away," he said. "I've got to look for something."

But the time would come when they would have to leave the Ship, step out into the frightening vastness of the planet—naked and afraid and shorn of the security of the enclosing shell that could be theirs no longer. But when that time came, he would know what to do. He was sure he would.

For when the men of Earth had planned so well, they would not have failed in the final moment to have left a letter of instructions for the starting over.

THE END

Made in the USA
Coppell, TX
07 June 2023